Bright and Early Books

Bright and Early Books are an offspring of the world-famous Beginner Books® . . . designed for an even lower age group. Making ingenious use of humor, rhythm, and limited vocabulary, they will encourage even pre-schoolers to discover the delights of reading for themselves.

For other Bright and Early titles, see the back endpapers.

Copyright © 2007 CCI Entertainment Ltd.
HARRY AND HIS BUCKET FULL OF DINOSAURS and all related characters and elements
are trademarks of and © CCI Entertainment Ltd.

All rights reserved.
Published in the United States by Random House Children's Books, a division
of Random House, Inc., New York.

BRIGHT & EARLY BOOKS and colophon and RANDOM HOUSE and colophon are
registered trademarks of Random House, Inc.

www.randomhouse.com/kids   www.harryandhisbucketfullofdinosaurs.com

Educators and librarians, for a variety of teaching tools,
visit us at www.randomhouse.com/teachers

Library of Congress Cataloging-in-Publication Data
Hooke, R. Schuyler.
X marks the spot / by R. Schuyler Hooke ; illustrated by Art Mawhinney. — 1st ed.
   p.   cm.
ISBN: 978-0-375-84141-5 (trade)
ISBN: 978-0-375-94243-3 (lib. bdg.)
I. Mawhinney, Art. II. Harry and his bucket full of dinosaurs (Television program).
III. Title.
PZ7.H76344Xm 2007   2006027136

Printed in the United States of America
10 9 8 7 6 5 4 3 2 1   First Edition

Harry AND HIS Bucket FULL of Dinosaurs

X Marks the Spot

Illustrated by
Art Mawhinney

Story by R. Schuyler Hooke
based on the Harry books
by Ian Whybrow and Adrian Reynolds

A Bright and Early Book
From BEGINNER BOOKS
A Division of Random House, Inc.

What is this beneath
my cap?
Who put this here?
It looks like a map!

This <u>is</u> a map that
we have got.
And look—an X!
X marks the spot!

Not just one X—
this map has more.
Some maps have one.
This map has four!

To Dino World we have to go.
What will we find?
We do not know!

1, 2, 3, JUMP!
We're on our way to
Dino World!

This X is near the
wishing well.
Can we find it?
Who can tell?

X marks the spot!

Where is the X? Do you see?
There it is! Up in that tree!

The X is much too high.
Oh, no!
Patsy can stretch her neck,
I know.

Go, Patsy! Go!

A puzzle piece!
What does it show?

Where is the next X?
The swamp is where!
It's muddy,
but we must go there.

X marks the spot!

Here we are.
Now look around. . . .
Look! An X.
There, on the ground.

The ground is muddy.
We will sink.
Pterence can fly it there,
I think!

Go, Pterence! Go!

Here's another piece to link.

Back to the map!
What should we do?
Another X! Another clue!

Where is this X?
Moo Mountain is where!
A long, high climb!
We must go there.

X marks the spot!

We climb and climb.
Oh, what a view!
But I don't see an X.
Do you?

Here it is, but it is stuck!
A rock is on it!
We're out of luck.
This rock is much too big
for me.

Taury can help to lift it free!
Go, Taury! Go!

Another piece.
What can it be?

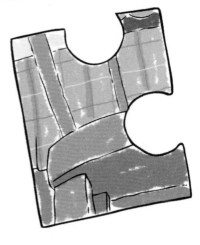

Back to the map.
There is one more.
The final X
is at the shore.

X marks the spot!

This hole is where an X
could hide.
And see,
an arrow points inside.

We must get in the hole,
but how?
Harry's arm fits in.
Oh, wow!

Go, Harry! Go!

We have all the pieces now!
All four pieces found!
How neat!

Our treasure puzzle
is complete!

But what is this?
I think I know!
It's back at home!
Come on, let's go!

We're home! Hooray!
Oh, look! It's there:
table, bowl, fan, and chair.

See the chair, the bowl,
the fan!

And look!
Here is a note from Nana!

Read us the note!
What does it say?

And what have we got
hidden here?
Oh, boy! Hip, hip, hooray!
Let's cheer!

Milk and cookies!
And fruit! What fun!
A yummy snack.
Our hunt is done!

That hits the spot!